ISBN 0 86112 824 9
© Brimax Books Ltd 1992. All rights reserved.
Published by Brimax Books Ltd, Newmarket, England 1992.
Second printing 1992.
Printed in Italy.

# The Jungle Book

Illustrated by Eric Kincaid

BRIMAX BOOKS · NEWMARKET · ENGLAND

# Introduction

Rudyard Kipling's *The Jungle Book* has delighted generations of children since it was first published in 1894. It tells the exciting story of Mowgli, the little boy brought up in the Indian jungle by a family of wolves.

After being accepted by the wolf pack on the word of Baloo the bear and Bagheera the black panther, Mowgli is taught the Law of the Jungle. He learns to respect the jungle and the creatures within it, but still manages to make a dangerous enemy of Shere Khan, the man-eating tiger.

Superbly illustrated by Eric Kincaid, this specially adapted version of *The Jungle Book* tells how Mowgli constantly out-wits Shere Khan. Younger readers will be enchanted by Mowgli's numerous adventures and fascinated by the animals he encounters deep within the mysterious Indian jungle.

# Contents

# Mowgli's Brothers

It was seven o'clock when Father Wolf woke up. Mother Wolf lay with her big grey nose dropped across her four tumbling, squealing cubs. "Augrh!" said Father Wolf. "It is time to hunt again."

He was about to spring out of the cave and down the hill when a little shadow with a bushy tail came up to the entrance. It was Tabaqui – the Jackal, and the wolves of India despise Tabaqui because he runs about making mischief and telling tales.

But they are afraid of him too, because Tabaqui, more than anyone else in the Jungle, is apt to go mad. Even the tiger runs and hides when little Tabaqui goes mad. We call it hydrophobia, or rabies, but the animals call it *dewanee* – the madness – and run.

"Enter then and look," said Father Wolf.

"How beautiful are your noble children!" said Tabaqui. "How large their eyes! Indeed, I might have remembered that the children of Kings are men from the beginning."

Now, Tabaqui knew as well as anyone else that

there is nothing as unlucky as complimenting children to their faces. He was pleased to see Mother and Father Wolf look uncomfortable.

Tabaqui sat there enjoying the mischief he had made, then he said spitefully, "Shere Khan, the Big One, has moved his hunting grounds. He has told me that he will hunt among these hills for the next month or so."

Shere Khan was the tiger who lived near the Waingunga River, twenty miles away.

"He has no right," Father Wolf began angrily. "By the Law of the Jungle, he has no right to change his quarters without due warning."

"His mother did not call him Lungri (the Lame One) for nothing," said Mother Wolf quietly. "He has been lame in one foot from his birth. That is why he has only killed cattle. Now the villagers of the Waingunga are angry with him!"

"Out, Tabaqui!" snapped Father Wolf. "Leave here and go and hunt with your master. You have done enough harm for one night."

"I'll go," said Tabaqui quietly. "But if you listen, you can hear Shere Khan below in the thickets."

Father Wolf listened and he heard the angry whine of a tiger who has caught nothing and doesn't care if all the Jungle knows it.

"The fool," said Father Wolf. "To begin a night's work with that noise! Does he think that our buck are like his fat Waingunga bullocks!"

"It is man that he hunts tonight," said Mother Wolf. The whine had changed to a sort of humming purr.

"Man!" said Father Wolf. "On our ground too?"

The Law of the Jungle, which never orders anything without a reason, forbids every beast to eat Man except when he is killing to show his children how to kill, and then he must hunt outside the hunting grounds of his pack or tribe. The real reason for this is that man-killing means, sooner or later, the arrival of men on elephants, with guns, and hundreds of men with gongs and rockets and torches.

The purr grew louder, and ended in the full-throated 'Aaarh' of the tiger's charge.

Then there was a howl – an untigerish howl – from Shere Khan.

Father Wolf ran out a few paces and heard Shere Khan muttering and mumbling savagely.

"The fool has had no more sense to jump at a woodcutter's camp-fire, and he has burned his feet," said Father Wolf.

"Something is coming uphill," said Mother Wolf, twitching one ear. "Get ready."

The bushes rustled a little in the thicket, and Father Wolf dropped with his haunches under him, ready for his leap. He made his bound before he saw what it was he was jumping at, and then he tried to stop himself. The result was that he shot up straight into the air for four or five feet, landing almost where he left the ground.

Directly in front of him stood a naked brown baby who could just walk, he looked up into Father Wolf's face and laughed.

"Is that a man's cub?" said Mother Wolf. "I have never seen one. Bring it here."

A wolf accustomed to moving his own cubs can, if necessary, mouth an egg without breaking it, and though Father Wolf's jaws closed right on the child's back, not a tooth even scratched the skin as he laid it down amongst the cubs.

The baby was pushing his way through the cubs to get close to the warm hide. "*Ahai*! He is taking his meal with the others," said Mother Wolf.

The moonlight was blocked out of the mouth of the cave, for Shere Khan's great square head and shoulders were thrust into the entrance.

"What does Shere Khan want?" asked Father Wolf, his eyes angry.

"A man's cub came this way," said Shere Khan. "Give it to me."

Father Wolf knew that the mouth of the cave was too narrow for the tiger to come in.

"The wolves are a free people," said Father Wolf. "They take orders from the head of the pack, not from any striped cattle-killer."

10

"By the bull that I killed, am I to stand nosing into your dog's den for what is rightly mine? It is I, Shere Khan, who speaks!"

"And it is I, Raksha (The Demon), who answers," said Mother Wolf. "The man's cub is mine, Lungri – mine to me! He shall not be killed. He shall live to run and hunt with the pack; and in the end, look you, hunter of little naked cubs – frog-eater – fish-killer – he shall hunt you! Now go away, go back to your mother, burned beast of the Jungle, lamer than when you came into the world! Go!"

Father Wolf looked on, amazed. He had almost forgotten the days when he had won Mother Wolf in a fair fight from five other wolves; the days when she ran in the Pack and was not called The Demon for compliment's sake. Shere Khan might have faced Father Wolf, but he could not stand up to Mother Wolf, for he knew that where he was, she had all the advantage of the ground and would fight to the death. So he backed out of the cave-mouth growling, and when he was clear he shouted, "Each dog barks in his own yard! We will see what the pack has to say about this fostering of man-cubs. The cub is mine, and to my teeth he will come in the end. Oh bush-tailed thieves!"

"Shere Khan speaks some truth," Father Wolf said, gravely. "The man-cub must be shown to the pack. Will you still keep him, Mother?"

"Keep him!" she gasped. "He came naked, by night, alone and very hungry; yet he was not afraid! Look, he has pushed one of my babes aside already. Keep him? Assuredly I will keep him. Lie still, little frog, Mowgli – for Mowgli the frog I will call you – the time will come when you will hunt Shere Khan as he has hunted you."

"But what will our Pack say?" said Father Wolf.

The Law of the Jungle states very clearly that any wolf may, when he marries, withdraw from the pack he belongs to; but as soon as his cubs are old enough to stand on their feet he must bring them to the Pack Council, which is generally held once a month at full moon, in order that the other wolves may identify them. After that inspection

the cubs are free to run where they please.

Father Wolf waited until his cubs could run a little, and then on the night of the pack meeting took them and Mowgli and Mother Wolf to the Council Rock – a hill top covered with stones and boulders where a hundred wolves could hide. Akela, the great grey Lone Wolf who led all the Pack by strength and cunning, lay out at full-length on his rock, and below him sat forty or more wolves of every size and colour. The Lone Wolf had led them for a year now.

There was very little talking at the rock. The cubs tumbled over each other in the centre of the circle and now and again a senior wolf would go quietly up to a cub, look at him carefully, and return to his place on noiseless feet. Akela from his rock would cry, "You know the Law – you know the Law. Look well, Oh Wolves!"

Father Wolf pushed 'Mowgli the Frog', as they called him, into the centre, where he sat laughing and playing with some pebbles that glistened in the moonlight. Akela never raised his head from his paws, but went on with the monotonous cry, "Look well!"

The voice of Shere Khan cried, "The cub is mine. Give him to me. What have the Free People to do with a man's cub?"

Akela never even twitched his ears, all he said was, "Look well, Oh Wolves! What have the Free People to do with the orders of any save the Free People? Look well!"

There was a chorus of deep growls, and a young wolf in his fourth year flung back Shere Khan's question to Akela, "What have the Free People to do with a man's cub?" Now, the Law of the Jungle lays down that if there is any dispute as to the right of a cub to be accepted by the Pack, he must be spoken for by at least two members of the Pack who are not his father and mother.

"Who speaks for this cub?" asked Akela.

The only other creature who is allowed at the Pack Council is Baloo, the sleepy brown bear who teaches the wolf-cubs the Law of the Jungle.

*"The cub is mine. Give him to me.*
*What have the Free People to do with a man's cub?"*

"The man's cub?" said Baloo. "I speak for the man's cub. I have no gift of words, but I speak the truth. Let him run with the Pack and be entered with the others. I myself will teach him."

"We need another to speak for the man's cub," said Akela. "Baloo has spoken and he is our teacher for the young cubs."

A black shadow dropped down into the circle. It was Bagheera the Black Panther. Everybody knew Bagheera, and nobody cared to cross his path.

"Oh Akela, and you, the Free People," he purred. "I have no say in your assembly; but the Law of the Jungle says that if there is a doubt in regard to a new cub, the life of that cub may be bought at a price. Am I right?"

"Good! Good!" said the young wolves, who were always hungry. "Listen to Bagheera. The cub can be bought for a price. It is the Law."

"Knowing that I have no right to speak here, I ask your permission to do so."

"Speak then," cried twenty voices.

"To kill a naked cub is a shame. Baloo has spoken on his behalf. Now to Baloo's words I will add one bull – a fat one, newly killed, not half a mile from here, if you will accept the man's cub according to the Law."

And then came Akela's deep bay, crying: "Look well – look well, Oh Wolves!"

Mowgli was still deeply interested in the pebbles and he did not notice when the wolves came and looked at him one by one. At last they all went down the hill for the dead bull, and only Akela, Bagheera, Baloo and Mowgli's own wolves were left. Shere Khan still roared in the night, for he was very angry that Mowgli had not been handed over to him.

"Go on, roar away," said Bagheera, under his whiskers. "For the time will come when this naked thing will make you roar to another tune, or I know nothing of Man."

"Men and their cubs are very wise," said Akela. "He may be a help in time."

"Truly, a help in a time of need; for none can

hope to lead the Pack forever," said Bagheera.

Akela said nothing. He was thinking of the time that comes to every leader of every pack when his strength goes from him and he gets weaker and weaker, until at last he is killed by his own wolves and a new leader comes up – to be killed in his turn.

"Take him away," he said to Father Wolf. "And train him as befits one of the Free People."

And that is how Mowgli was entered into the Seeonee Wolf-Pack at the price of a bull and on Baloo's good word.

Now we must skip ten or eleven whole years. Father Wolf taught Mowgli the meaning of things in the Jungle, until every rustle in the grass and every breath of the warm night air meant just as much to him as the work in an office means to a business man. When he was not learning, he sat out in the sun and slept. When he felt dirty or hot he swam in the forest pools; and when he wanted honey (Baloo told him that honey and nuts were just as pleasant to eat as raw meat) he climbed for it, and that Bagheera showed him how to do. Bagheera would lay out on a branch and call, "Come along, Little Brother," and at first Mowgli would cling like a sloth, but afterwards he would fling himself through the branches almost as boldly as the grey ape.

He took his place at the Council Rock, too, when the Pack met, and there he discovered that if he stared hard at any wolf, the wolf would be forced to drop his eyes. At other times he would pick the long thorns out of the pads of his friends. He would go down the hillside and look very curiously at the villagers in their hunts.

He loved better than anything else to go with Bagheera into the dark, warm heart of the forest, to sleep all through the drowsy day, and at night to see how Bagheera did his killing. As soon as he was old enough to understand things, Bagheera told him that he must never touch cattle because he had been bought into the Pack at the price of a bull's life. "All the Jungle is yours," said Bagheera.

15

"You can kill everything that you are strong enough to kill; but for the sake of the bull that bought you, you must never kill or eat any cattle young or old. That is the Law of the Jungle."

Mother Wolf told him that Shere Khan was not to be trusted, and that some day he would have to kill Shere Khan; but though a young wolf would have remembered that advice every hour, Mowgli forgot it because he was only a boy – though had he been asked, he would have called himself a wolf if he had been able to speak in any human tongue.

Shere Khan was always crossing his path in the Jungle, for as Akela grew older and weaker the lame tiger had become great friends with the younger wolves of the Pack, who followed him for scraps, something that Akela would never have allowed if he had dared push his authority to the proper bounds.

Bagheera, who had eyes and ears everywhere, knew something of this, and once or twice he told Mowgli in so many words that Shere Khan would kill him some day; and Mowgli would laugh and answer,

"I have the pack and I have you; and Baloo, even though he is so lazy, might strike a blow or two for my sake. Why should I be afraid?"

It was a very warm day that a new notion came to Bagheera – born of something that he had heard. Perhaps Ikki the Porcupine had told him; but he said to Mowgli when they were deep in the Jungle, "Little Brother, how often have I told you that Shere Khan is your enemy?"

"As many times as there are nuts on that palm," said Mowgli. "What of it? I am sleepy, Bagheera, and Shere Khan is all long tail and loud talk."

"But this is no time for sleeping. Tabaqui has told you too."

"Ho! Ho!" said Mowgli. "Tabaqui came to me not long ago with some rude talk that I was a naked man's cub; but I caught Tabaqui and swung him twice against a palm tree to teach him better manners."

"That was a stupid thing to do, he would have told you something that concerns you. Open those eyes, Little Brother. Shere Khan would not dare to kill you in the Jungle; but remember, Akela is very old and soon the day will come when he cannot kill his buck, and then he will be leader no more. Many of the wolves that looked you over when you were first brought to the Council are old too, and the young wolves believe, as Shere Khan has taught them, that a man-cub has no place with the Pack. In a little while you will be a man."

"And what is a man that he should not run with his brothers?" said Mowgli. "I was born in the Jungle. I have obeyed the Law of the Jungle, and there is no wolf of ours from whose paws I have not pulled a thorn. Surely they are my brothers!"

Bagheera stretched himself out at full length and half shut his eyes. "Little Brother," he said. "Feel under my jaw."

Mowgli put up his strong brown hand, and just under Bagheera's silky chin, where the giant rolling muscles were all hidden by the glossy fur, he found a little bald spot.

"No one in the Jungle knows that *I*, Bagheera, carry the mark of the collar. It was because of this that I paid the price for you at the Council when you were a little naked cub. Yes, I too was born among men. I had never seen the Jungle. They fed me behind bars from an iron pan until one night I felt that I was Bagheera – the Panther – and no man's play thing, and I broke the silly lock with one blow of my paw and escaped. As I had learned the way of men, I became more terrible in the Jungle than Shere Khan. Is it not so?"

"Yes," said Mowgli, "all the Jungle fear Bagheera – all except Mowgli."

"Oh, you are a man's cub," said the Black Panther, very tenderly; "and even as I returned to my Jungle, so you must go back to your real home – to the men who are your brothers – if you are not killed in the Council."

"But why should any wish to kill me?" said Mowgli.

"Look at me," said Bagheera; and Mowgli looked at him steadily between the eyes. The big panther

17

turned his head away after half a minute.

"That is why," he said, shifting his paw on the leaves. "Even I cannot look you between the eyes, and I was born among men, and I love you, Little Brother. The others hate you because their eyes cannot meet yours – because you are wise – because you have pulled thorns from their feet – because you are a man."

"I did not realise," said Mowgli sullenly.

"What is the Law of the Jungle? Strike first then speak. By your very carelessness they know that when Akela misses his next kill – and at each hunt it costs him more to pin the buck – the Pack will turn against him and against you. They will hold Jungle Council at the Rock, and then – and then – I have it!" said Bagheera, leaping up. "Quickly, go down to the men's huts in the valley, and take some of the Red Flower which they grow there, so that when the time comes you will have a stronger friend than even I or Baloo or those of the Pack that love you. Get the Red Flower."

By the Red Flower Bagheera meant fire, only no creature in the Jungle will call fire by its proper name. Every beast lives in deadly fear of it.

"The Red Flower?" said Mowgli. "I've seen it growing outside their huts in the twilight. I will get some."

"There speaks the man's cub," said Bagheera proudly. "Remember that it grows in little pots. Get one swiftly, and keep it near you ready for when you need it."

"Right," said Mowgli. "I'll go. Oh my Bagheera – " he slipped his arm around the splendid neck, and looked deep into the big eyes – "are you sure that all this is Shere Khan's doing?"

"By the Broken Lock that freed me, I am sure, Little Brother."

"Then I will pay Shere Khan for this," said Mowgli; and he bounded away.

"Oh Shere Khan, there was never a blacker day of hunting than that frog-hunt of yours ten years ago!" said Bagheera to himself.

18

Mowgli ran through the forest, he plunged downward through the bushes, to the stream at the bottom of the valley. There he stopped, for he heard the sound of the Pack hunting, heard the bellow of a hunted sambhur. Then there were wicked howls from the younger wolves. "Akela! Akela! Let the Lone Wolf show his strength. Spring, Akela!"

The Lone Wolf must have sprung and missed his hold, for Mowgli heard the snap of his teeth and then a yelp as the sambhur knocked him over with his forefoot.

He did not wait to hear any more, but ran on; and the yells grew fainter behind him as he ran into the croplands where the villagers lived.

"Bagheera was right," he panted. "Tomorrow is an important day for Akela and for me."

Then he pressed his face close to the window and watched the fire on the hearth. He saw the husband-man's wife get up and feed it in the night with black lumps; and when the morning came, he saw the man's child pick up a pot, fill it with lumps of red-hot charcoal, put it under his blanket, and go out to tend the cows in the byre.

"Is that all?" said Mowgli. "If a cub can do it, there is nothing to fear." So he strode round the corner and met the boy, took the pot from his hand, and disappeared into the mist while the boy howled in fear.

"They are very like me," said Mowgli, blowing into the pot, as he had seen the woman do. "This thing will die if I do not give it things to eat," and he dropped twigs and dried bark on the red stuff. Half-way up the hill he met Bagheera with the morning dew shining like moonstones on his coat.

"Akela has missed," said the Panther. "They would have killed him last night, but they needed you too."

"I was among the ploughed lands. I am ready. See!" Mowgli held up the fire-pot.

"Good! Now I have seen men put a dry branch into that stuff, and soon the Red Flower blossoms at the end of it. Are you not afraid?"

"No, why should I be scared? I remember now – if it isn't a dream – how, before I was a wolf, I lay beside the Red Flower, and it was warm and pleasant."

All that day Mowgli sat in the cave tending his fire-pot. Tabaqui came to the cave and told him rudely enough that he was wanted at the Council Rock.

Akela, the Lone Wolf lay by the side of his rock as a sign that the leadership of the Pack was open. Bagheera lay close to Mowgli, and the fire-pot was between Mowgli's knees. When they were all gathered together, Shere Khan began to speak – a thing he would never have dared to do when Akela was in his prime.

"He has no right," whispered Bagheera. "Say so. He is a dog's son. He will be frightened."

Mowgli sprang to his feet. "Free People," he cried. "Since when does Shere Khan lead the Pack? What has a tiger to do with our leadership?"

There were yells of, "Silence man's cub! Let him speak. He has kept our Law," until at last the seniors of the Pack thundered, "Let the Dead Wolf speak." When the leader of the Pack has missed his kill, he is called the Dead Wolf for as long as he lives, which generally is not for long.

Akela raised his old head wearily.

"Free People, and you too, jackals of Shere Khan. For many seasons I have led you to and from the kill. Now I have missed my kill. You know how the plot was made. You know how you brought me up to an untried buck to make my weakness known. Your right is to kill me here on the Council Rock now. Therefore, I ask, who comes to make an end of the Lone Wolf?"

There was a long hush, for no single wolf cared to fight Akela to the death. Then Shere Khan roared, "What have we to do with this toothless fool? He is doomed to die! It is the man-cub who has lived too long. Give him to me. I am weary of this man-wolf folly. He has troubled the Jungle for ten seasons. He is a man's child, and from the marrow of my bones I hate him!"

Then more than half the Pack yelled: "A man! A man! What has a man to do with us? Let him go to his own place."

Akela lifted his head again, and said: "He has eaten our food. He has slept with us. He has driven game for us. He has broken no word of the Law of the Jungle."

"Also, I paid for him with a bull when he was accepted. The worth of a bull is little, but Bagheera's honour is something he will perhaps fight for," said Bagheera, in his gentlest voice.

"A bull that was paid for ten years ago!" the Pack snarled. "What do we care for ten year old bones?"

"He is our brother in all but blood," Akela went on, "Some of you are eaters of cattle, and under Shere Khan's teaching, go by dark and snatch children from the villager's doorstep. Therefore I know you are cowards. I promise that if you let the man-cub go to his own place, I will not, when my time comes to die, bare one tooth against you. I cannot do more than this, but if you want, I can save you the shame of killing a brother against whom there is no fault, a brother spoken for and bought into the Pack according to the Law of the Jungle."

"He is a man!" snarled the Pack; and most of the wolves began to gather round Shere Khan, whose tail was beginning to twitch.

"It's up to you now, Mowgli," said Bagheera to the boy. "We can do no more except fight."

Mowgli stood up – the fire-pot in his hands. Then he stretched out his arms, and yawned in the face of the Council; but he was furious with rage and sorrow, for, wolf-like, the wolves had never told him how they hated him. "Listen you!" he cried. "There is no need for this dog's jabber. You have told me so often tonight that I am a man, that I feel your words are true. So I do not call you my brothers any more, but *sag* (dogs), as a man would. What you will do and what you will not do, is not up to you. It is up to me; and so we will see all the matter more clearly, I, the man, have brought with me a little of the Red Flower which you fear."

21

He flung the fire-pot on the ground, and some of the red coals lit a tuft of dried moss that flared up. All the Council drew back in terror before the leaping flames.

Mowgli thrust his dead branch into the fire until the twigs lit and crackled, and then whirled it above his head.

"You are now the master," said Bagheera softly. "Save Akela from death. He was always your friend."

Akela, the grim old wolf who had never asked for mercy in his life, gave one piteous look at Mowgli as the boy stood all naked, his long black hair tossing over his shoulders in the light of the blazing branch that made the shadows jump and quiver.

"Good!" said Mowgli, staring round slowly. "I see that you are dogs. I go from you to my own people. The Jungle is closed to me, and I must forget your talk and your companionship; but I will be more merciful than you are. Because I was all but your brother in blood, I promise that when I am a man among men I will not betray you to men as you have betrayed me." He kicked the fire with his foot, and the sparks flew up. "There shall be no war between any of us and the Pack. But there is a debt to pay before I go." He strode forward to where Shere Khan sat blinking stupidly at the flames, and caught him by the tuft on his chin.

"Up, dog!" Mowgli cried. "Up when a man speaks, or I will set that coat ablaze!"

Shere Khan's ears lay flat back against his head, and he shut his eyes, for the blazing branch was very near.

"This cattle-killer said he would kill me in the Council because he could not kill me when I was a cub. Here's how we beat dogs when we are men. Move a whisker, Lungri, and I will ram the Red Flower down your throat!" He beat Shere Khan over the head with the branch, and the tiger whimpered and whined in an agony of fear.

"Pah! Singed jungle-cat – go now! But remember next time I come to the Council Rock, as a man should come, it will be with Shere Khan's hide on my head. For the rest, Akela goes free to live as he pleases. You will not kill him, because that is not my will. Nor do I think that you will sit here any longer. So! Go!" The fire was burning furiously at the end of the branch, and Mowgli struck right and left round the circle, and the wolves ran howling with sparks burning their fur.

At last there were only Akela, Bagheera and perhaps ten wolves that had taken Mowgli's part. Then something began to hurt Mowgli inside him, as he had never been hurt in his life before, and he caught his breath and sobbed, and the tears ran down his face.

"What is it?" he said. "I don't want to leave the Jungle, and I don't know what this is. Am I dying, Bagheera?"

"No, Little Brother. Those are only tears such as men use," said Bagheera. "Now I know you are a man, and a man's cub no longer. The Jungle is indeed closed to you from now on. Let them fall, Mowgli. They are only tears." So Mowgli sat and cried as though his heart would break.

"Now," he said. "I will go to men. But first I must say farewell to my Mother." He went to the cave where she lived with Father Wolf, and he cried on her coat, while the four cubs howled miserably.

"You will not forget me?" said Mowgli.

"Never while we can follow a trail," said the cubs. "Come to the foot of the hill when you are a man, and we will talk to you."

"Come soon," said Father Wolf. "For we are old, your mother and I."

"Come soon," said Mother Wolf. "Little naked son of mine, for listen, child of man, I loved you more than I ever loved my cubs."

"I will surely come," said Mowgli. "When I come it will be to lay out Shere Khan's hide on the Council Rock. Tell them in the Jungle never to forget me!"

The dawn was beginning to break when Mowgli went to meet those mysterious things called men.

# Kaa's Hunting

The story of Kaa and Mowgli happened before Mowgli was turned out of the Seeonee Wolf-Pack. It was in the days when Baloo was teaching him the Law of the Jungle. The big brown bear was delighted to have so quick a pupil, for the young wolves will only learn as much of the Law of the Jungle that applies to their own pack and tribe, and run away as soon as they can repeat the Hunting Verse, "Feet that make no noise; eyes that can see in the dark; ears that can hear the wind in their lairs, and sharp white teeth, all these things are the marks of our brothers except Tabaqui the Jackal and the Hyena whom we hate." But Mowgli had to learn a great deal more than this.

Sometimes Bagheera, the black panther, would come lounging through the Jungle to see how his pet was getting on, and would purr while Mowgli repeated the day's lesson to Baloo. The boy could climb almost as well as he could swim, and swim almost as well as he could run; so Baloo taught him the Wood and Water Laws; how to tell a rotten branch from a safe one; how to speak politely to the wild bees when he came across a hive of them fifty feet above ground; what to say to Mang the Bat when he disturbed him in the branches at midday. Then, he was taught the Stranger's Hunting Call, which must be repeated aloud till it is answered, whenever one of the Jungle-People hunts outside his own grounds. It means, translated, "Give me permission to hunt here because I am hungry", and the answer is, "Hunt then for food, but not for pleasure".

Baloo said to Bagheera, one day when Mowgli had been cuffed and run off in a temper, "A man-cub is a man-cub, and he must learn all the Law of the Jungle."

"But think how small he is," said the black panther. "How can his little head carry all of your talk?"

"Is there anything in the Jungle too little to be killed? No. That is why I teach him these things, and that is why I hit him, very softly, when he forgets."

"Softly!" Bagheera grunted. "His face is all bruised today by your – softness."

"Better to be bruised from head to foot by me who loves him than that he should come to harm through knowing no better," Baloo answered very earnestly. "I am now teaching him the Master-Words of the Jungle that shall protect him from the birds and the Snake-People, and all that hunt on four feet, except his own pack. He can now claim protection, if he will only remember the words, from all in the Jungle. Is that not worth a little beating?"

"But what are those Master-Words? I am more likely to give help than to ask it," Bagheera stretched out one paw and admired the steel-blue talons – "still I should like to know."

"I will call Mowgli and he shall say them – if he will. Come Little Brother!"

"My head is ringing like a bee-tree," said a sullen little voice above their heads, and Mowgli slid down a tree trunk very angry and hurt, adding as he reached the ground, "I come for Bagheera and not for you, fat old Baloo!"

"Tell Bagheera, then, the Master-Words of the Jungle that I have taught you today," said Baloo.

"Master-Words for which people?" said Mowgli. "The Jungle has many tongues. I know them all."

"You know a little, but not much. Say the word for the Hunting-People then – great scholar."

"We be of one blood, you and I," said Mowgli, giving the words the bear accent which all the Hunting-People use.

"Good, now for the birds."

Mowgli repeated, with the Kite's whistle at the end of the sentence.

"Now for the Snake-People," said Bagheera.

The answer was a perfect hiss, and Mowgli kicked up his feet behind, clapped his hands together to applaud himself, and jumped on to Bagheera's back, where he sat sideways, drumming with his heels on the glossy skin.

"There, that was worth a little bruise," said the brown bear tenderly. "Some day you will remember me." Then he turned to tell Bagheera how he had begged the Master-Words from Hathi the Wild Elephant, who knows all about these things, and how Hathi had taken Mowgli down to a pool to get the Snake Word from a water-snake, because Baloo could not pronounce it, and how Mowgli was now reasonably safe against all accidents in the Jungle, because neither snake, bird, nor beast would hurt him.

"No-one then is to be feared," Baloo wound up, patting his big furry stomach with pride.

"Except his own tribe," said Bagheera, under his breath; and then aloud to Mowgli, "Have a care for my ribs, Little Brother! What is all this dancing up and down?"

Mowgli had been trying to make himself heard by

pulling at Bagheera's fur and kicking hard. "And so I shall have a tribe of my own and lead them through the branches all day long," shouted Mowgli.

"What is this new folly?" said Bagheera.

"Yes, and throw branches and dirt at old Baloo," Mowgli went on. "They have promised me this. Ah!"

Baloo's big paw scooped Mowgli off Bagheera's back.

"Mowgli," said Baloo. "You have been talking with the *Bandar-log* – the Monkey People."

Mowgli looked at Bagheera. His eyes were as hard as jade-stones.

"You have been with the Monkey-People. That is great shame."

"When Baloo hurt my head," said Mowgli. "I went away and the grey apes came down from the trees and had pity on me."

"The pity of the Monkey-People!" Baloo snorted. "The stillness of the mountain stream! The cool of the summer sun! There is no such thing!"

"And then they gave me nuts and pleasant things to eat, and they – they carried me in their arms up to the top of the trees and said I should be their leader some day!"

"They have no leader," said Bagheera. "They have always lied."

"They were very kind and told me to come again. Why have I never been taken among the Monkey-People? They stand on their feet as I do. They do not hit me with hard paws. They play all day."

"Listen, Man-cub," said the bear, and his voice rumbled like thunder on a hot night. "I have taught you all the Law of the Jungle for all the peoples of the Jungle – except the Monkey-Folk who live in the trees. They have no Law. They are outcasts. They have no speech of their own, but use the stolen words they overhear when they listen. Their way is not our way. They are without leaders. The falling of a nut turns their minds to laughter. We of the Jungle have no dealing with them. Have you ever heard me speak of the *Bandar-log* before today?"

*"And so I shall have a tribe of my own,
and lead them through the branches all day long."*

"No," said Mowgli, in a whisper for the forest was very quiet now Baloo had finished.

"We do not notice even when they throw nuts and filth on our heads."

He had hardly spoken when a shower of nuts and twigs spattered down through the branches.

"The Monkey-People are forbidden," said Baloo. "Forbidden to the Jungle-People. Remember." A fresh shower came down on their heads and the two friends trotted away, taking Mowgli with them.

What Baloo had said about the monkeys was perfectly true. They belonged to the tree-tops, and as beasts very seldom look up, there was no reason for the monkeys and the Jungle-People to cross each other's paths.

The Monkey-People would throw nuts and twigs at beasts in the hope of being noticed. They were always just about to have a leader, but they never did, because their memories would not hold over from one day to the next, so they compromised things by saying, "What the *Bandar-log* thinks now the Jungle will think later." This comforted them a great deal. They were very pleased when Baloo was angry about Mowgli playing with them. They never meant to do any more but one of them invented what seemed to him a brilliant idea, and he told the others that Mowgli would be a useful person to keep in the tribe, because he could weave sticks together for protection against the wind, so if they caught him, they could make him teach them. This time, they said, they were really going to have a leader and become the wisest people in the Jungle – so wise that everyone else would notice and envy them. Therefore they followed Baloo, Bagheera and Mowgli very quietly till it was time for the midday nap, and Mowgli, who was very much ashamed of himself, slept between the panther and the bear, resolving to have no more to do with the Monkey-People.

The next thing he remembered was feeling hands on his legs and arms and then a swash of branches in his face, and then he was staring down through the swaying boughs as Baloo awoke the Jungle with his

deep cries and Bagheera bounded up the trunk with every tooth bared. The *Bandar-log* howled with triumph and scuffled away to the upper branches where Bagheera dared not follow, shouting, "He has noticed us, Bagheera has noticed us!" Then they began their flight, and the flight of the Monkey-People through tree-land is one of the things that nobody can describe. They have their regular roads and crossroads, uphills and downhills, and by these they can travel even at night if necessary. Two of the strongest monkeys caught Mowgli under the arms and swung off with him through the tree-tops. Sick and giddy as Mowgli was, he could not help enjoying the wild rush, though the glimpses of the earth far down below frightened him. Sometimes he could see for miles across the still green Jungle, as a man on top of a mast can see for miles across the sea. So bounding and crashing and whooping and yelling, the whole tribe of *Bandar-log* swept along the tree-roads with Mowgli as their prisoner.

For a time he was afraid of being dropped; then he grew angry but knew better than to struggle, and then began to think. The first thing was to send back word to Baloo and Bagheera, for, at the speed the monkeys were going, he knew his friends would be left far behind. It was useless to look down, for he could only see the top-sides of the branches, so he stared upward and saw Chil the Kite balancing and wheeling as he kept watch over the Jungle waiting for something to die. Chil saw that the monkeys were carrying something, and dropped a few hundred yards to find out whether their load was good to eat. He whistled with surprise when he saw Mowgli being dragged up to a tree-top and heard him give the Kite-call for, "We be of one blood, you and I." The waves of the branches closed over the boy, but Chil balanced away to the next tree in time to see the little brown face come up again. "Mark my trail," Mowgli shouted. "Tell Baloo of the Council Rock."

"In whose name, Brother?" Chil had never seen Mowgli before, though he had heard of him.

"Mowgli, the Frog. Man-cub they call me! Mark my trail!"

Chil nodded and rose up till he looked no bigger than a speck of dust.

"They never go far," he said with a chuckle. "They never do what they set out to do."

So he rocked on his wings, his feet gathered up under him, and waited.

Meantime, Baloo and Bagheera were furious with rage and grief. Bagheera climbed as he had never climbed before, but the thin branches broke beneath his weight, and he slipped down, his claws full of bark.

"Why did you not warn the man-cub?" he roared to poor Baloo.

"Quickly! Oh, quickly! We – we may still catch them!" Baloo panted.

"At that speed. It would not tire a wounded cow. Teacher of the Law – cub-beater! Sit still and think! Make a plan. This is no time for chasing. They may drop him if we follow too close."

"*Arrula! Whoo!* They may have dropped him already, being tired of carrying him. Who can trust the *Bandar-log*? Oh, Mowgli! Why did I not warn you against the Monkey-Folk, now perhaps I have knocked the day's lesson out of his mind, and he will be alone without the Master-Words."

Baloo clasped his hands over his ears and rolled to and fro moaning.

"At least he gave me all the words correctly a little time ago," said Bagheera impatiently. "Unless and until they drop him from the branches in sport, or kill him out of idleness, I have no fear for the man-cub. He is wise and well taught, and above all he has the eyes that make the Jungle-People afraid. But (and it is a great evil) he is in the power of the *Bandar-log*, and they, because they live in the trees, have no fear of any of our people."

"Fool that I am," said Baloo, uncurling with a jerk. "It is true what Hathi, the Wild Elephant says: "To teach his own fear"; and they, the *Bandar-log*, fear Kaa the Rock Snake. He can climb

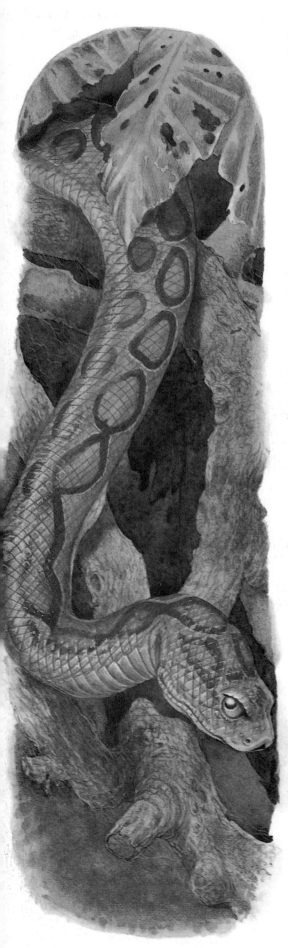

as well as they can. He steals the young monkeys in the night. The whisper of his name makes their little tails cold. Let us go to Kaa."

"What will he do for us? He is not of our tribe, being footless – and with most evil eyes," said Bagheera.

"He is very old and very cunning. Above all, he is always hungry," said Baloo, hopefully.

"He sleeps for a full month after he has eaten. He may be asleep now, and even if he were awake, he may prefer to kill his own goats." Bagheera, who did not know much about Kaa, was naturally suspicious.

"Then in that case, you and I together, old hunter might make him see sense." Here Baloo rubbed his faded brown shoulder against the panther, and they went off to look for Kaa the Rock Python.

They found him stretched out on a ledge in the afternoon sun, admiring his beautiful new coat, for he had been in retirement for the last ten days, changing his skin, and now he was very splendid.

"He has not eaten," said Baloo, with a grunt of relief, as soon as he saw the beautifully mottled yellow-and-brown jacket. "Be careful, Bagheera! He is always a little blind after he has changed his skin, and very quick to strike."

Kaa was not a poisonous snake – in fact he rather despised the poisonous snakes as cowards – but his strength lay in his hug, and when he lapped his huge coils around anybody there was no more to be said. "Good hunting!" cried Baloo.

"Good hunting for us all!" Kaa answered. "Oho, Baloo, what do you want here? Good hunting, Bagheera! One of us at least needs food. Is there any news of game afoot?"

"We are hunting," said Baloo carelessly. He knew that you must not hurry Kaa. He is too big.

"Give me permission to come with you," said Kaa. "A blow more or less is nothing to either of you, Bagheera or Baloo, but I have to wait for days and days in the woodpath and climb half a night on the mere chance of a young ape. Pss-haw! The branches are not what they were when I was young. Rotten twigs and dry boughs are they all."

"Maybe your great weight has something to do with the matter," said Baloo.

"I am a fair length," said Kaa, with a little pride. "I came very near to falling on my last hunt, the noise of my slipping woke the *Bandar-log*, and they called me the most evil names."

"Footless, yellow earthworm," said Bagheera.

"Sss! Have they ever called me that?" said Kaa.

"Something of that kind it was that they shouted to us last moon, but we never noticed them. They will say anything – even that you have lost all your teeth, and dare not face anything bigger than a kid, because (they are indeed shameless, these *Bandar-log*) – because you are afraid of the he-goat's horns," Bagheera went on sweetly.

Now a snake, especially a wary old python like Kaa, very seldom shows that he is angry, but Baloo and Bagheera could see the big swallowing muscles on either side of Kaa's throat ripple and bulge.

"The *Bandar-log* have shifted their grounds," he said quietly. "When I came up into the sun today I heard them whooping among the tree-tops."

"It is the *Bandar-log* that we follow now," said Baloo; but the words stuck in his throat, for that was the first time in his memory that one of the Jungle-People had owned to being interested in the doings of the monkeys.

"Beyond doubt then it is no small thing that takes two such hunters – leaders in their own Jungle I am certain – on the trail of the *Bandar-log*," Kaa replied courteously, as he swelled with curiosity.

"Indeed," Baloo began. "I am the Teacher of the Law to the Seeonee wolf-cubs, and Bagheera here . . ."

"Is Bagheera," said the black panther, for he did not believe in being humble. "Those nut-stealers have stolen away our man-cub, of whom you have perhaps heard."

"I heard some news that a man-thing was entered

33

into a wolf-pack, but I did not believe it."

"But it is true. He is such a man-cub as never was," said Baloo. "The best and wisest and boldest of man-cubs – my own pupil, and besides, Kaa, we love him."

"Our man-cub is in the hands of the *Bandar-log* now, and we know that of all the Jungle-People they fear Kaa alone," said Bagheera.

"They fear me alone. They have good reason," said Kaa. "A man-thing in their hands is in no good luck and is not to be envied. They called me also – 'yellow fish', was it not?"

"Earthworm," said Bagheera. "As well as other things which I cannot say now for shame."

"We must remember them to speak well of their master. Aa-sh! Now where did they go with the cub?"

"The Jungle alone knows. Towards the sunset I believe," said Baloo. "We thought you may know, Kaa."

"Up! Up! Up! Up! Hillo! Illo! Illo! Look up, Baloo of the Seeonee Wolf-Pack!"

Baloo looked up to see where the voice came from, and there was Chil the Kite. He had ranged all over the Jungle looking for the bear and had missed him in the thick foliage.

"What is it?" said Baloo.

"I have seen Mowgli among the *Bandar-log*. He asked me to tell you. The *Bandar-log* have taken him beyond the river to the monkey city – to the Cold Lairs. They may stay there for a night, ten nights, or an hour. I have told the bats to watch through the dark. Good hunting, all you below!"

"Full gorge and a deep sleep to you, Chil," cried Bagheera. "I will remember you in my next kill, and put aside the head for you alone."

"It is nothing. The boy spoke the Master-Word. I could have done no less," and Chil circled up again to his roost.

"He has not forgotten to use his tongue," said Baloo, with a chuckle of pride. "To think of one so young remembering the Master-Word for the birds while he was being pulled across the trees!"

"It was most firmly driven into him," said Bagheera. "Now we must go to the Cold Lairs."

They all knew where it was, but few of the Jungle-People ever went there. The monkeys lived there as much as they could be said to live anywhere, and no self-respecting animal would come within eyeshot of it except in times of drought, when the half-ruined tanks and reservoirs held a little water.

"It is half a night's journey – at full speed," said Bagheera.

Baloo looked very serious. "I will go as fast as I can," he said anxiously.

"We dare not wait for you. Follow, Baloo. We must go on the quick-foot – Kaa and I."

"Feet or no feet, I can keep abreast of all your four," said Kaa shortly. Baloo made one effort to hurry, but had to sit down panting, and so they left him to come on later, while Bagheera hurried forward, at the quick panther-canter. Kaa said nothing, but, strive as Bagheera might, the huge Rock Python held level with him.

"By the Broken Lock that freed me," said Bagheera, when twilight had fallen. "You are by no means slow!"

"I am hungry," said Kaa.

In the Cold Lairs the Monkey-People were not thinking of Mowgli's friends at all. They had brought the boy to the Lost City, and were very pleased with themselves for doing it. Mowgli had never seen an Indian city before, and though this was almost a heap of ruins it seemed very wonderful and splendid. Trees had grown into and out of the walls; the battlements were tumbled down and decayed.

A great roofless palace crowned the hill, and the marble of the courtyards and the fountains were split, and stained with red and green. From the palace you could see the rows and rows of roofless houses that made up the city looking like empty honeycombs filled with blackness; the shapeless block of stone that had been an idol, in the square where the four roads met.

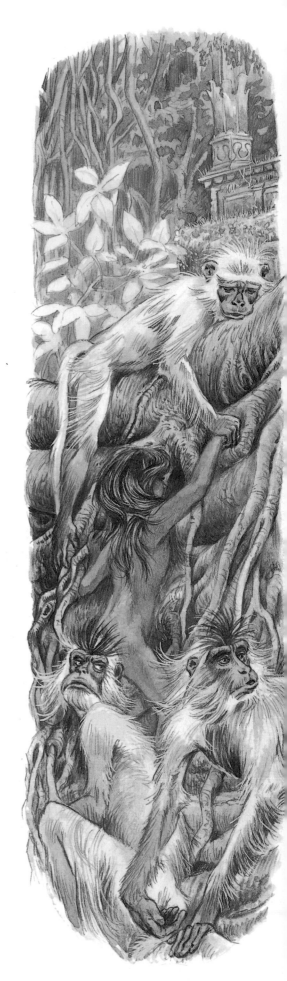

*Trees had grown into and out of the walls;*
*the battlements were tumbled down and decayed.*

The monkeys called the place their city, and pretended to despise the Jungle-People because they lived in the forest. And yet they never knew what the buildings were made for, nor how to use them. They would sit in circles on the floor of the king's council chamber, and scratch for fleas and pretend to be men; or they would run in and out of the roofless houses and collect pieces of plaster and old bricks in a corner, and forget where they had hidden them. They explored all the passages and dark tunnels in the palace and the hundreds of little dark rooms, but they never remembered what they had seen and what they had not. They drank at the tanks and made the water all muddy, and then they fought over it. Then all would begin again till they grew tired of the city and went back to the tree-tops, hoping the Jungle-People would notice them.

Mowgli, who had been trained under the Law of the Jungle, did not like or understand this kind of life. The monkeys dragged him into the Cold Lairs late in the afternoon, and instead of going to sleep, they joined hands and danced about and sang their foolish songs. One of the monkeys made a speech and told his companions that Mowgli's capture marked a new thing in the history of the *Bandar-log*, for Mowgli was going to teach them how to weave sticks and canes together as protection against rain and cold. Mowgli picked up some creepers and began to work them in and out, and the monkeys tried to imitate; but in a very few minutes they lost interest.

"I wish to eat," said Mowgli. "I am a stranger in this part of the Jungle. Bring me food, or give me permission to hunt here."

Twenty or thirty monkeys bounded away to bring him nuts and wild papaws; but they fell to fighting on the road, and it was too much trouble to go back with what was left of the fruit. Mowgli was sore and angry as well as hungry.

"All that Baloo said about the *Bandar-log* is true," he thought to himself. "They have no Law, no Hunting Call, and no leaders – nothing but

foolish words and little picking, thievish hands. So if I am starved or killed here, it will be all my own fault. But I must try to return to my own Jungle. Baloo will surely beat me, but that is better than chasing silly rose-leaves with the *Bandar-log*."

No sooner had he walked to the city wall than the monkeys pulled him back. He set his teeth and said nothing, but went with the shouting monkeys to a terrace above the red sandstone reservoirs that were half-full of rain water. Sore, sleepy and hungry as he was, Mowgli could not help laughing when the *Bandar-log* began, twenty at a time to tell him how great and wise and strong and gentle they were, and how foolish he was to wish to leave them.

"We are great, we are free. We are the most wonderful people in all the Jungle! We all say so, and so it must be true," they shouted. "Now, as you are a new listener and can carry our words back to the Jungle-People so that they may notice us in the future, we will tell you all about our most excellent selves."

Mowgli made no objection, and the monkeys gathered by hundreds and hundreds on the terrace to hear their own speakers singing the praises of the *Bandar-log*. Mowgli nodded and blinked, and said "Yes" when they asked him a question, and his head spun with the noise. "Tabaqui the Jackal must have bitten all these people," he said to himself. "Now they have the madness. Do they never go to sleep? Now there is a big cloud coming to cover that moon. If it were only a big enough cloud I might try to run away in the darkness. But I am tired."

That same cloud was being watched by two good friends in the ditch below the city wall, for Bagheera and Kaa, knowing well how dangerous the Monkey-People were in large numbers, did not wish to run any risks. The monkeys never fight unless they are a hundred to one, and few in the Jungle care for those odds.

"I will go to the west wall," whispered Kaa, "and

come down swiftly with the slope in my favour.
They will not throw themselves upon my back in
their hundreds, but . . ."

"I know," said Bagheera. "If only Baloo were
here; but we must do what we can. When that cloud
covers the moon I shall go to the terrace. They
are holding some sort of council over the boy."

"Good hunting!" Kaa said grimly, and he glided
away to the west wall. The big snake was delayed
a while before he could find a way up the stones.
The cloud hid the moon, and as Mowgli wondered
what would come next he heard Bagheera's light
feet on the terrace. The black panther had raced
up the slope almost without making a sound and was
striking right and left among the monkeys, who
were seated round Mowgli in circles fifty and
sixty deep. There was a howl of fright and rage,
and then as Bagheera tripped on the rolling
kicking bodies beneath him, a monkey shouted,
"There is only one here! Kill him!"

A scuffling mass of monkeys, biting, scratching,
tearing and pulling, closed over Bagheera. Another
five or six laid hold of Mowgli, dragged him up
the wall of the summer-house and pushed him
through the hole of the broken dome. A man-trained
boy would have been badly bruised, for the fall
was a good fifteen feet, but Mowgli fell as Baloo
had taught him to fall, and landed on his feet.

"Stay there," shouted the monkeys. "Till we have
killed your friend, and later we will play with
you – if the Poison-People leave you alive."

"We be of one blood, you and I," said Mowgli,
quickly giving the Snake's Call. He could hear rustling
and hissing in the rubbish all around him and gave
the call a second time, to make sure.

"Even ssso! Down hoods all!" said half a dozen
low voices. "Stand still, Little Brother, for your
feet may do us harm."

Mowgli stood as quietly as he could, peering
through the open-work and listening to the furious
din of the fight round the black panther. For the
first time since he was born, Bagheera was
fighting for his life.

39

"Baloo must be at hand; Bagheera would not have come alone," Mowgli thought; and then he called aloud: "To the tank, Bagheera! Roll and plunge! Get to the water!"

Bagheera heard, and the cry that told him that Mowgli was safe gave him new courage. He worked his way desperately, inch by inch, straight for the reservoirs, hitting in silence. Then from the ruined wall nearest the Jungle rose up the rumbling war-shout of Baloo. The old bear had done his best, but he could not get there sooner.

"Bagheera!" he shouted. "I am here, I climb! I haste! *Ahuwora*! The stones slip under my feet! Wait my coming, Oh, most infamous *Bandar-log*!" He panted up the terrace only to disappear to the head in a wave of monkeys, but he threw himself squarely on his haunches, and, spreading out his forepaws, hugged as many as he could hold, and then began to hit with a regular *bat-bat-bat*, like the flipping strokes of a paddle-wheel. A crash and a splash told Mowgli that Bagheera had fought his way to the tank where the monkeys could not follow. The panther lay gasping for breath, his head just out of the water, while the monkeys stood three deep on the red steps, dancing up and down with rage, ready to spring upon him from all sides if he came out to help Baloo.

It was then that Bagheera lifted up his dripping chin, and in despair gave the Snake's Call for protection – "We be of one blood, you and I" – for he believed that Kaa had turned tail at the last minute. Even Baloo, half smothered under the monkeys on the edge of the terrace, could not help chuckling as he heard the black panther asking for help.

Kaa had only just worked his way over the west wall, landing with a wrench that dislodged a coping-stone into the ditch. He had no intention of losing any advantage of the ground, and coiled and uncoiled himself once or twice, to be sure that every foot of his long body was in working order. Meanwhile the fight with Baloo went on, and the monkeys yelled in the tank around Bagheera,

*"Bagheera!"* he shouted, *"I am here, I climb! I haste!*
*Ahuwora! Wait my coming, most infamous Bandar-log!"*

and Mang the Bat, flying to and fro, carried the news of the great battle over the Jungle. Then Kaa came straight, quickly, and anxious to kill. The fighting-strength of a python is in the driving blow of his head backed by all the strength and weight of his body. His first stroke, delivered into the heart of the monkeys meant that there was no need for a second. The monkeys scattered with cries of – "Kaa! It is Kaa! Run! Run! Run!"

Generations of monkeys had been scared into good behaviour by the stories their elders told them of Kaa, who could slip across the branches as quietly as moss grows, and steal away the strongest monkeys that ever lived. Kaa was everything the monkeys feared in the Jungle. And so they ran, stammering with terror, to the walls and roofs of the houses, and Baloo drew a deep breath of relief. His fur was much thicker than Bagheera's but he had suffered sorely in the fight. Then Kaa opened his mouth for the first time and spoke one long hissing word, and the far-away monkeys, hurrying to the defence of the Cold Lairs, stayed cowering where they were. Then the clamouring broke out again. The monkeys leaped higher up the walls and shrieked as they skipped across the battlements.

"Get Mowgli out of that trap; I can do no more," Bagheera gasped. "Let us take Mowgli and go. They may attack again."

"They will not move until I let them," Kaa hissed, and the city was silent once more.

"I think they may have pulled me into a hundred little bearlings," said Baloo gravely, shaking one leg after the other. "Kaa, we owe you, I think, our lives – Bagheera and I."

"No matter, where is the manling?"

"Here in a trap, I cannot climb out," cried Mowgli.

"Take him away. He dances like Mao the Peacock. He will crush our young," said the cobras inside.

"Hah!" said Kaa, with a chuckle. "He has friends everywhere, this manling. Stand back, manling; and take cover, Oh Poison-People. I am going to break

42

down the wall."

Kaa looked carefully until he found a discoloured crack in the marble tracery showing a weak spot, then, lifting up six feet of his body clear of the ground, sent home smashing blows, nose first. The screen-work broke and fell away and Mowgli leaped through the opening and flung himself between Baloo and Bagheera.

"Are you hurt?" asked Baloo, hugging him softly.

"I am sore and hungry, and not a little bruised; but oh, they have been much tougher with you my Brothers! You're bleeding!"

"Others also," said Bagheera licking his lips, and looking round at the monkey-dead on the terrace and round the tank.

"It's nothing, if only you are safe. Oh my pride of all little frogs!" whimpered Baloo.

"Of that we shall judge later," said Bagheera in a voice that Mowgli did not at all like. "But here is Kaa, to whom we owe the battle and to whom you owe your life. Thank him according to our customs, Mowgli."

Mowgli turned and saw the great python's head swaying a foot above his own.

"We be of one blood, you and I," Mowgli said. "I take my life from you, tonight. My kill shall be your kill if ever you are hungry, Oh Kaa."

"All thanks, Little Brother," said Kaa, though his eyes twinkled. "And what may so bold a hunter kill? I ask that I may follow when next he goes abroad."

"I kill nothing – I am too little – but I drive goats towards such as can use them. I have some skill in these," he held out his hands. "If you are ever in a trap, I may pay the debt which I owe to you, to Bagheera and to Baloo. Good hunting to you all, my masters."

"Well said," growled Baloo. The python dropped his head lightly for a moment on Mowgli's shoulder. "A brave heart and a courteous tongue," said Kaa. "They shall carry you far through the Jungle. But now go quickly with your friends. For I don't think you should see what follows."

The moon was sinking behind the hills, and the lines of trembling monkeys huddled together on the walls looked like ragged, shaky things. Kaa glided out to the centre of the terrace and brought his jaws together with a ringing snap that drew all the monkeys' eyes upon him.

"Good. Now begins the Dance of the Hunger of Kaa. Sit still and watch," said Kaa.

He turned twice or three times in a big circle, weaving his head from left to right. Then he began making loops and figures of eight with his body, and soft, oozy triangles that melted into squares and five-sided figures, and coiled mounds, never resting, never hurrying, and never stopping his low, humming song. It grew darker and darker, till at last the dragging shifting coils disappeared, but they could hear the rustle of the scales.

"*Bandar-log*," said Kaa at last, "Can you move without my say so? Speak!"

"Without your order we cannot move, Oh Kaa."

"Good! Come one pace closer to me."

The lines of monkeys swayed forward helplessly, and Baloo and Bagheera took one stiff step forward with them.

"Closer!" hissed Kaa, and they all moved again.

Mowgli layed his hands on Baloo and Bagheera, and the two beasts started as though they had been woken from a dream.

"Keep your hand on my shoulder," Bagheera whispered. "Or I must go back to Kaa."

"It is only Kaa making circles in the dust," said Mowgli. "Let us go." The three slipped off through a gap in the walls to the Jungle.

"*Whoof*!" said Baloo, when he stood under the still trees again. "Never again will I make an ally of Kaa," and he shook himself all over.

"He knows more than we," said Bagheera, trembling. "In a little time had I stayed, I should have walked down his throat. All this came of your playing with the *Bandar-log*."

"True, it is true," said Mowgli sorrowfully. "I am an evil man-cub, and my stomach is sad in me."

"What does the Law of the Jungle say, Baloo?"

"Being sorry never stops a punishment. But remember, Bagheera, he is very little," said Baloo.

"I will remember, but he has done mischief, and blows must be dealt."

Bagheera gave him half a dozen love taps; from a panther's point of view they would hardly have waked one of his cubs, but to a seven-year-old boy they amounted to as severe a beating as you could wish to avoid. When it was all over Mowgli sneezed, and picked himself up without a word.

"Now," said Bagheera, softly. "Jump on my back."

The beauty of Jungle Law is that punishment settles all scores. There is no nagging after. Mowgli laid his head down on Bagheera's back and slept so deeply that he didn't even wake up when he was put down by Mother Wolf's side in the cave.

His spots are the joy of the Leopard; his horns
    are the Buffalo's pride.
Be clean, for the strength of a hunter is known by
    the gloss of his hide.
If you find that the bullock can toss you, or the
    heavy-browed sambhur can gore;
You need not stop work to inform us: we knew it
    ten seasons before.
Oppress not the cubs of the stranger, but hail
    them as Sister and Brother,
For though they are little and fubsy, it may be
    the Bear is their mother.
"There is none like to me!" says the Cub in the
    pride of his earliest kill;
But the Jungle is large and the Cub he is small,
    Let him think and be still.

Maxims of Baloo

45

# "Tiger! Tiger!"

Now we must go back to the first tale. When Mowgli
left the wolf's cave after the fight with the Pack
at the Council Rock, he went down to the ploughed
lands where the villagers lived, but he would not
stop there because it was too near the Jungle. He
hurried on, till he came to a country that he did
not know. The valley opened up into a great plain
dotted over with rocks and cut up by ravines. At
one end stood a little village, and at the other
end the thick Jungle came down in a sweep to the
grazing-grounds, and stopped there as though it
had been cut off with a hoe. All over the plain,
cattle and buffalo were grazing, and when the
little boys in charge of the herds saw Mowgli they
shouted and ran away, and the yellow pariah dogs
that hang about every Indian village barked.
Mowgli walked on, for he was feeling hungry, and
when he came to the village gate he saw the big
thorn-bush that was drawn up before the gate at
twilight pushed to one side.

  "Umph!" he said, for he had come across more than
one such barricade in his night rambles after

46

things to eat. "So men are afraid of the People of the Jungle here also." He sat down by the gate, and when a man came out he stood up, opened his mouth, and pointed down it to show he wanted food. The man stared, and ran back up the one street of the village shouting for the priest. The priest came to the gate, and with him at least a hundred people, who stared and talked and shouted and pointed at Mowgli.

"What is there to be afraid of?" said the priest. "Look at the marks on his arms and legs. They are the bites of wolves. He is but a wolf-child run away from the Jungle."

"To be bitten by wolves, poor child," said two or three women together. "By my honour, Messua, he is not unlike your boy that was taken by the tiger."

"Let me look," said a woman with heavy copper rings on her wrists and ankles, and she peered at Mowgli under the palm of her hand. "Indeed he is not. He is thinner, but he has the very look of my boy."

The priest was a very clever man, and he knew that Messua was wife to the richest man in the village. "What the Jungle has taken the Jungle has restored. Take the boy into your house, my sister," he said.

"By the Bull that bought me," said Mowgli to himself. "All this talking is like another looking over by the Pack! Well, if I am a man, a man I must become."

The crowd parted as the woman beckoned Mowgli to her hut. She gave him a long drink of milk and some bread, and then she laid her hand on his head and looked into his eyes; for she thought that perhaps he might be her real son come back from the Jungle where the tiger had taken him. So she said, "Nathoo, Oh, Nathoo!" Mowgli did not show that he knew the name. "Don't you remember the day when I gave you your new shoes?" She touched his foot, and it was almost as hard as horn. "No," she said sorrowfully, "those feet have never worn shoes, but you are very like my Nathoo, and you shall be my son."

*"Let me look," said a woman with heavy copper rings
on her wrists and ankles.*

Mowgli was uneasy, "What is the good of a man," he thought, "if he does not understand man's talk? Now I am as silly and dumb as a man would be with us in the Jungle. I must learn their talk."

As soon as Messua pronounced a word Mowgli would imitate it almost perfectly, and before dark he had learned the names of many things in the hut.

But there was a problem at bedtime, because Mowgli would not sleep under anything that looked so like a panther-trap as that hut, and when they shut the door he went out through the window.

"Leave him alone," said Messua's husband. "Remember he has probably never slept on a bed. If he has indeed been sent in the place of our son he will not run away."

So Mowgli stretched himself in some long, clean grass at the edge of the field, but before he had closed his eyes a soft grey nose poked him under the chin.

"Phew!" said Grey Brother (he was the eldest of Mother Wolf's cubs). "This is a poor reward for following you twenty miles. You smell of wood-smoke and cattle – altogether like a man already."

"Are all well in the Jungle?" said Mowgli, hugging him.

"All except the wolves that were burned by the Red Flower. Now, listen. Shere Khan has gone away to hunt far off till his coat grows again, for he is badly singed. When he returns he swears that he will lay your bones in the Waingunga. When I come down here again, I will wait for you in the bamboos at the edge of the grazing-ground."

For three months after that night Mowgli hardly ever left the village gate, he was so busy learning the ways and customs of men. First he had to wear a cloth round him, which annoyed him horribly; and then he had to learn about money and about ploughing, of which he did not see the use. Then the little children in the village made him very angry. Luckily, the Law of the Jungle had taught him to keep his temper; but when they made fun of him, only the knowledge that it was

unsportsmanlike to kill little naked cubs kept him from picking them up and breaking them in two.

He did not know his own strength in the least. In the Jungle he knew he was weak compared with the beasts but in the village people said he was as strong as a bull.

The priest told Messua's husband that Mowgli had better be set to work as soon as possible; and the village head-man told Mowgli that he would have to go out with the buffaloes next day, and herd them while they grazed. No one was more pleased than Mowgli. That night, because he had been appointed, as it were, a servant of the village, he went off to a circle that met every evening. It was the village club, and the head-man and the watchman and the barber (who knew all the gossip of the village), and old Buldeo, the village hunter, who owned a Tower musket, met and smoked. The old men sat around the tree and talked till far into the night. They told wonderful tales and Buldeo told even more wonderful ones about the ways of beasts in the Jungle. Most of the tales were about animals, for the Jungle was always at their door.

Mowgli, who, naturally, knew something of what they were talking of, had to cover his face not to show that he was laughing, while Buldeo, the Tower musket across his knees climbed on from one wonderful story to another, and Mowgli's shoulders shook.

Buldeo was explaining how the tiger that had carried away Messua's son was a ghost-tiger, and his body was inhabited by the ghost of a wicked old money-lender, who had died some years ago.

"And I know that this is true," he said, "because Purun Dass always limped from the blow he got in a riot when his account books were burned, and the tiger that I speak of, he limps, too, for the tracks of his pads are unequal."

"Are all these tales such cobwebs and moon-talk?" said Mowgli. "That tiger limps because he was born lame, as everyone knows."

Buldeo was speechless with surprise for a moment, and the head-man stared.

"Oho! It is the Jungle brat, is it?" said Buldeo.

Mowgli rose to go. "All evening I have lain here listening," he called back over his shoulder, "and, except once or twice, Buldeo has not said one word of truth concerning the Jungle, which is at his very door. How, then, shall I believe the tales of ghosts and gods and goblins which he says he has seen?"

"It is full time that boy went into herding," said the head-man, while Buldeo puffed and snorted at Mowgli's impertinence.

The custom of most Indian villages is for a few boys to take the cattle and buffaloes out to graze in the early morning, and bring them back at night; and the very cattle that would trample a white man to death allow themselves to be banged and bullied and shouted at by children that hardly came up to their noses. So long as the boys keep with the herds they are safe, for not even the tiger will charge a mob of cattle. But if they straggle to pick flowers or hunt lizards, they are sometimes carried off. Mowgli went through the village street in the dawn, sitting on the back of Rama, the great herd bull; and the buffaloes rose out of their byres one by one, and followed him.

An Indian grazing-ground is all rocks and scrubs and tussocks and little ravines, among which the herds scatter and disappear. The buffaloes generally keep to the pools and muddy places, where they lie wallowing in the warm mud for hours. Mowgli drove them on to the edge of the Jungle; then he dropped from Rama's neck, trotted off to a bamboo clump, and found Grey Brother.

"Ah!" said Grey Brother. "I have waited here very many days."

"What news of Shere Khan?" said Mowgli.

"He has come back to this country, and has waited here a long time for you. Now he has gone off again, for game is scarce. But he means to kill you."

"Very good," said Mowgli. "So long as he is away, will you or one of the four brothers sit on that rock, so that I can see you as I come out of the

51

village. When he comes back, wait for me in the ravine by the *dhâk*-tree in the centre of the plain. We need not walk into Shere Khan's mouth."

Then Mowgli picked out a shady place, and lay down and slept, while the buffaloes grazed around him.

The children sing long songs with odd native quavers at the end of them, and the days seem longer than most peoples' whole lives. Then evening comes, and the children call, and the buffaloes lumber up out of the sticky mud, and they all string along the plain back to the twinkling village lights.

Day after day, Mowgli would lead the buffaloes out to their wallows, and day after day he would see Grey Brother's back a mile and a half away across the plain (so he knew that Shere Khan had not come back), and day after day he would lay on the grass listening to the noises around him, and dream of old days in the Jungle.

At last a day came when he did not see Grey Brother at the signal-place, and he laughed and headed the buffaloes for the ravine by the *dhâk*-tree, which was covered with golden-red flowers. There sat Grey Brother, every bristle on his back lifted.

"He has hidden for a month to throw you off guard. He crossed the ranges last night with Tabaqui, hotfoot on your trail," said the wolf, panting.

Mowgli frowned. "I am not afraid of Shere Khan, but Tabaqui is very cunning."

"Have no fear," said Grey Brother, licking his lips a little. "I met Tabaqui in the dawn. Now he is telling all his wisdom to the kites, but he told *me* everything before I broke his back. Shere Khan's plan is to wait for you at the village gate this evening – for you and for no one else. He is lying up now in the big, dry ravine of the Waingunga."

"Has he eaten today, or does he hunt empty?" said Mowgli, for the answer meant life or death to him.

"He killed at dawn – a pig – and he has drunk

52

too. Remember, Shere Khan could never fast, even for the sake of revenge."

"Oh! Fool, fool! What a cub's cub it is! Eaten and drunk too, and he thinks that I shall wait till he has slept! Now, where does he lie up? These buffaloes will not charge unless they wind him, and I cannot speak their language. Can we get behind his tracks so that they may smell it?"

"He swam far down the Waingunga to cut that off," said Grey Brother.

"Tabaqui told him that, I know. He would never have thought of it alone," Mowgli sat thinking. "The big ravine of the Waingunga opens out on the plain not half a mile from here. I can take the herd round through the Jungle to the head of the ravine and then sweep down – but he would slink out at the foot. We must block that end. Grey Brother, can you cut the herd in two for me?"

"Not I, perhaps – but I have brought a wise helper." Grey Brother trotted off and dropped into a hole. There lifted up a huge grey head that Mowgli knew well, and the hot air was filled with the most desolate cry of all the Jungle – the hunting-howl of a wolf at midday.

"Akela! Akela!" said Mowgli, clapping his hands. "I might have known that you would not forget me. We have a job to do. Cut the herd in two, Akela. Keep the cows and calves together, and the bulls and the plough-buffaloes by themselves."

The two wolves ran, ladies'-chain fashion, in and out of the herd, which snorted and threw up its head, and separated into two clumps. In one the cow-buffaloes stood, with their calves in the centre, and glared and pawed, ready, if a wolf would only stay still, to charge down and trample the life out of him. In the other, the bulls and the young bulls snorted and stamped; but, though they looked more imposing, they were much less dangerous, for they had no calves to protect. No six men could have divided the herd so neatly.

"What orders?" panted Akela.

Mowgli slipped onto Rama's back. "Drive the bulls away to the left, Akela. Grey Brother, when we are

53

*The two wolves ran, ladies'-chain fashion, in and out of the herd,*
*which snorted and threw up its head, and separated into two clumps.*

gone, hold the cows together, and drive them into the foot of the ravine."

"How far?" said Grey Brother, panting and snapping.

"Till the sides are higher than Shere Khan can jump," shouted Mowgli. "Keep them there till we come down." The bulls swept off as Akela bayed, and Grey Brother stopped in front of the cows. They charged down on him and he ran just before them to the foot of the ravine, as Akela drove the bulls far to the left.

"Well done! Another charge and they are fairly started. Careful, now – careful, Akela. A snap too much, and the bulls will charge. Did you think these creatures could move so swiftly?" Mowgli called.

"I have hunted these too in my time," gasped Akela in the dust. "Shall I turn them into the Jungle?"

"Yes, turn! Swiftly turn them! Rama is mad with rage. If only I could tell them what I need of them today!"

The bulls were turned to the right this time, and crashed into the standing thicket. The other herd-children, watching with the cattle half a mile away, hurried to the village as fast as their legs could carry them, crying that the buffaloes had gone mad and run away.

But Mowgli's plan was simple enough. All he wanted to do was make a big circle uphill and get at the head of the ravine, and then take the bulls down it and then catch Shere Khan between the bulls and the cows; for he knew that after a meal and a full drink Shere Khan would not be in any condition to fight or to clamber up the side of the ravine. He was soothing the buffaloes now by voice, and Akela dropped far to the rear, only whimpering once or twice to hurry the rear-guard. It was a long circle, for they did not wish to get too near the ravine and give Shere Khan warning. At last Mowgli rounded up the bewildered herd at the head of the ravine on a grassy patch that sloped down to the ravine itself. Mowgli looked at the sides of the ravine, and he saw with a great deal of satisfaction that they ran nearly straight up and down and would give no foothold to a tiger who wanted to get out.

"Let them breathe, Akela," he said. "They have not winded him yet. I must tell Shere Khan who comes. We have him in the trap."

He put his hands to his mouth and shouted down the ravine.

After a long time there came back the drawling, sleepy snarl of a full-fed tiger just wakened.

"Who calls?" said Shere Khan, and a splendid peacock fluttered up out of the ravine screeching.

"I, Mowgli. Cattle-thief, it is time to come to the Council Rock! Down – hurry them down, Akela! Down Rama! Down!"

The herd paused for an instant on the edge of the slope, but Akela gave tongue in the full hunting-yell, and they pitched over one after the other. Once started, there was no chance of stopping, Rama caught the smell of Shere Khan and bellowed.

"Ha! Ha!" said Mowgli, on his back. "Now you know!"

The buffaloes knew what business was before them – the terrible charge of the buffalo-herd against which no tiger can hope to stand. Shere Khan heard the thunder of their hooves and lumbered down the ravine, looking for some way to escape; but the walls of the ravine were straight, and he had to keep on, heavy with his dinner and his drink, willing to do anything rather than fight. The herd splashed through the pool he had just left, bellowing till the narrow ravine rang. Mowgli heard an answering bellow from the foot of the ravine, saw Shere Khan turn (the tiger knew if the worst came to the worst it was better to meet the bulls than the cows with their calves), and then Rama tripped, and went on over something soft, and, with the bulls at his heels, crashed full into the other herd. That charge carried both herds out into the plain. Mowgli slipped off Rama's neck, laying about him right and left with his stick.

"Quick, Akela! Break them up! Scatter them, or they will be fighting one another. Drive them away, Akela. *Hai*, Rama! *Hai*! Softly now, softly."

Akela and Grey Brother ran to and fro nipping the buffaloes' legs, and though the herd wheeled once to charge up the ravine again, Mowgli managed to turn Rama, and the others followed him to the wallows.

Shere Khan needed no more trampling. He was dead.

"Brothers, that was a dog's death," said Mowgli, feeling for the knife he always carried in a sheath around his neck now that he lived with men. "But he would never have shown fight. His hide will look well on the Council Rock."

A boy trained among men would never have dreamed of skinning a ten-foot tiger alone, but Mowgli knew better than anyone else how an animal's skin is fitted on.

Presently a hand fell on his shoulder, and looking up he saw Buldeo, with the Tower musket. The children had told the village about the buffalo stampede, and Buldeo went out angrily, only too anxious to correct Mowgli for not taking better care of the herd. The wolves dropped out of sight as soon as they saw the man coming.

"What is this folly?" said Buldeo angrily. "To think that you can skin a tiger! Where did the buffaloes kill him? It is the Lame Tiger, too, and there is a hundred rupees on his head. Well, we will overlook you letting the herd run off, and perhaps I will give you one of the rupees as a reward when I have taken the skin to Khanhiwara."

"Hum!" said Mowgli, half to himself as he ripped back the skin of a forepaw. "So you will take the skin to Khanhiwara for the reward, and perhaps give me one rupee? Now as far as I'm concerned, I need the skin for my own use."

"How can you talk this way to the chief hunter of the village? Your luck and the stupidity of your buffaloes have helped you to this kill."

"By the Bull that bought me," said Mowgli, who was trying to get at the shoulder, "Here Akela, this man plagues me."

Buldeo, who was still stooping over Shere Khan's head, found himself sprawling on the grass, with a grey wolf standing over him, while Mowgli went on skinning as if he were alone in all India.

"Ye-es," he said, between his teeth. "You are absolutely right, Buldeo. You will never give me one anna of this reward. There is an old war between this lame tiger and myself – a very old war, and – I have won."

"Maharaj! Great King!" Buldeo said at last, in a husky whisper.

"Yes," said Mowgli, without turning his head, chuckling a little.

"I am an old man. I did not know you were anything more than a herd-boy. May I rise up and go away, or will your servant tear me to pieces?"

"Go, and peace be with you. Only, another time do not meddle with my game. Let him go, Akela."

Buldeo hobbled away to the village as fast as he could, looking back over his shoulder in case Mowgli should turn into something terrible.

Mowgli went on with his work, but it was nearly twilight before he and the wolves had drawn the great, bright skin away from the body.

"Now we must hide this and take the buffaloes home! Help me to herd them, Akela."

The herd rounded up in the misty twilight, and when they got near the village Mowgli saw lights, and heard the conches and bells blowing and banging. Half the village seemed to be waiting for him by the gate. "That is because I have killed Shere Khan," he said to himself; but a shower of stones whistled by his ears, and the villagers shouted: "Sorcerer! Wolf's brat! Jungle-demon! Go away! Get away from here quickly. Shoot Buldeo, shoot!"

The old Tower musket went off with a bang, and a young buffalo bellowed in pain.

"What is the matter," said Mowgli, as the stones flew thicker.

"They are not unlike the Pack, these brothers of yours," said Akela, sitting down composedly. "It is in my head that they would cast you out!"

"Wolf! Wolf's cub! Go away!" shouted the priest.

"Again? Last time it was because I was a man. This time it is because I am a wolf. Let us go, Akela."

A woman – it was Messua – ran across to the herd, and cried: "Oh, my son, my son! They say you are a sorcerer who can turn himself into a beast at will. I do not believe, but go away or they will kill you. Buldeo says you are a wizard, but I know that you have avenged Nathoo's death."

"Come back, Messua!" shouted the crowd. "Come back, or we will stone you, too."

Mowgli laughed a little short ugly laugh, for a stone had hit him in the mouth. "Run back, Messua. This is one of the foolish tales they tell under the big tree at dusk. I have at least paid for your son's life. Farewell; and run quickly, for I shall send the herd in more swiftly than their brickbats. I am no wizard, Messua. Farewell!"

"Now, once more, Akela," he cried. "Bring the herd in."

The buffaloes were anxious enough to get into the village. They hardly needed Akela's yell, but charged through the gate like a whirlwind, scattering the crowd left and right.

"Fare you well, children of men, and thank Messua that I do not come in with my wolves and hunt you up and down your street."

He turned on his heels and walked away with the Lone Wolf. "No more sleeping in traps for me, Akela. Let us get Shere Khan's skin and go away."

When the moon rose over the plain, the horrified villagers saw Mowgli, with two wolves at his heels and a bundle on his head, trotting across at the steady wolf's trot that eats up the miles like fire.

The moon was just going down when Mowgli came to the Council Rock, they stopped at Mother Wolf's cave.

"They have cast me out of the Man-Pack, Mother," shouted Mowgli, "but I have come with the hide of Shere Khan to keep my word." Mother Wolf walked stiffly from the cave with the cubs behind her, and her eyes glowed as she saw the skin.

"I told him on that day, when he crammed his head and shoulders into this cave, hunting for you, Little Frog – I told him that the hunter would be hunted. It is well done."

"Little Brother, it is well done," said a voice from the thicket. "We were lonely in the Jungle without you," and Bagheera came running to Mowgli's bare feet. Mowgli spread the skin out on the flat rock where Akela used to sit, and pegged it down. Akela lay down upon it, and called the old call to the Council, "Look well, Oh Wolves!"

Ever since Akela had been deposed, the Pack had been without a leader, hunting and fighting at their own pleasure. But they answered the call from habit, and some of them were lame from the traps they had fallen into, and some limped from shot-wounds, and some were mangy from eating bad food, and many were missing; but they came to the Council Rock, and saw Shere Khan's striped hide on the Rock, and the huge claws dangling at the end of the empty, dangling feet. It was then that Mowgli made up a song without any rhymes, a song that came up into his throat all by itself, and he shouted it aloud, leaping up and down on the rattling skin.

"Look Well, Oh Wolves! Have I kept my word?" said Mowgli, and one tattered wolf howled: "Lead us again, Oh Akela. Lead us again, Oh man-cub, we want to be the Free People once more."

"Nay," purred Bagheera. "That may not be. When you are well fed, the madness may come upon you again. Not for nothing are you called the Free People. You fought for freedom, and it is yours. Eat it, Oh Wolves."

"Man-Pack and Wolf-Pack have cast me out," said Mowgli. "Now I will hunt alone in the Jungle."

"And we will hunt with you," said the four cubs.

So Mowgli went away and hunted with the four cubs in the Jungle from that day on. But he was not always alone, because years afterwards he became a man and married.

But that is a story for grown-ups.

61